Your Future as a COSMETOLOGIST

HIGH-DEMAND CAREERS™

Your Future as a COSMETOLOGIST

RACHEL GIVEN-WILSON AND SALLY GANCHY

Rosen YA™
New York

Published in 2020 by The Rosen Publishing Group, Inc.
29 East 21st Street, New York, NY 10010

First Edition

Library of Congress Cataloging-in-Publication Data

Names: Given-Wilson, Rachel, author. | Ganchy, Sally, author.
Title: Your future as a cosmetologist / Rachel Given-Wilson and Sally Ganchy.
Description: New York : Rosen Publishing, 2020. | Series: High-demand careers | Includes bibliographical references and index.
Identifiers: LCCN 2018047703| ISBN 9781508187806 (library bound) | ISBN 9781508187790 (pbk.)
Subjects: LCSH: Beauty culture—Vocational guidance—Juvenile literature.
Classification: LCC TT958.23 .G58 2020 | DDC 646.7/2023—dc23
LC record available at https://lccn.loc.gov/2018047703

Manufactured in the United States of America

Contents

Introduction

From the beginning of time, people have found ways to alter their appearances using what we now call cosmetics. People in ancient Egypt lined their eyes with kohl and painted their eyelids green with a mineral called malachite. In ancient China, as early as 3000 BC, kings and queens alike painted their nails using gold and silver nail polish made of gum arabic, beeswax, egg whites, gelatin, and vegetable dyes. In eighteenth-century France, members of the nobility wore elaborate powdered wigs adorned with ribbons, bows, and even small sculptures of birds and ships!

Across the world, people use style to express themselves. From hairstyles to makeup and nail art, cosmetologists help people to show the world who they are.

In the United States, trends in hair and makeup often go hand in hand with changes in society. In the 1920s, as women were gaining rights and freedoms, they expressed their liberation by cutting their hair into short bobs. In the 1950s, elaborate hairdos were all the rage. Held in place with lots of styling products, these hairdos could be seen to symbolize a return to normal life after the hardship of World War II. In the 1960 and '70s, hippies grew their hair long to express their desire for a more natural lifestyle.

Today, the range of options for how to wear hair, nails, and makeup seems limitless. People use style to make a statement about who they are and to express different parts of themselves. Some people get their hair, makeup, and nails done professionally for special occasions, such as a wedding or prom. For others, visiting the nail salon is a regular part of their self-care routine. Some people even use makeup to change the way they express their gender—makeup is no longer considered "just for girls," as the popularity of shows like *RuPaul's Drag Race* illustrates. Who has the power to assist in these transformations? Cosmetologists!

Cosmetologists are professionals who are trained in the art of hair styling, skin care, makeup application, hair removal, or other beauty-related treatments. Cosmetologists are creative people who like to work with their hands. It helps to have an outgoing personality since many clients enjoy chatting while they have their hair or nails done. Many cosmetologists work in salons and spas, some work privately, and others end up opening their own salons. If you love inventing new hairstyles, painting your friends' nails, and figuring out which treatments make your skin glow, you may be cut out for a career as a cosmetologist. There are steps you can start taking now to prepare for your career!

Chapter 1

WHAT DOES IT TAKE TO BE A COSMETOLOGIST?

If you're someone who loves doing hair and nails and spending time figuring out which products fit your skin type, you may be considering a career as a cosmetologist. Working in the beauty industry can be hard work, but it's also a job that can come with a lot of flexibility. As long as you have the right personality for it and you're willing to put in the time to learn the required skills, being a cosmetologist can be an extremely rewarding career.

DO YOU HAVE WHAT IT TAKES?

As a cosmetologist, you'll be working with people all day, listening to them, talking to them, and learning about them. In fact, building relationships with clients is an important part of growing your business. If your clients enjoy your company, they'll be more likely to use your services again. You must be enthusiastic, outgoing, friendly, compassionate, diplomatic, and energetic.

Cosmetologists are creative, and they work with their hands. If you excel at sculpture, painting, design, or other arts, you'll find that those skills will serve you well as a cosmetologist. For instance, hairdressers need the eye of a sculptor as they cut and shape hair. Colorists and makeup artists need a painter's understanding of color.

If you work in the beauty industry, it's important to have people skills and enjoy conversation. Many clients like to chat while they get their hair or nails done.

It's also important to have an interest in fashion. Clients often rely on their hairstylists to keep their look updated. Makeup artists are asked to provide fresh makeup ideas for special events.

A cosmetologist must be clean and organized. You must be willing to work quickly and efficiently so that you don't waste time during an appointment. You should be a self-starter, especially if you hope to start your own business.

OPTIONS FOR TRAINING

The journey toward becoming a cosmetologist begins with finding the right training. There are a number of different options, depending on your interests and goals. There are vocational high schools across the country where students can start their cosmetology training before they get their high school diploma. However, these students will still need to complete some training after high school and earn a cosmetology license before going to work as a cosmetologist.

It is also possible to train as a cosmetologist at a college or university. At a college or university, you can learn cosmetology while taking advantage of a wider variety of educational opportunities. Colleges and universities may also offer more options for financial aid.

The most common route to becoming a cosmetologist is to enroll in cosmetology school, which is also known as beauty school. In many states, you must have graduated from high school or earned a GED to go to cosmetology school. Check the requirements in your state.

Some students opt to go to a school that only covers their specific area of interest. Therefore, you may hear aspiring beauty professionals talk about going to nail school, esthetician school, hair school, barbering school, electrolysis school, or makeup school.

COSMETOLOGY SCHOOLS AND BEAUTY SCHOOLS

Cosmetology schools and beauty schools teach students the science and theory behind cosmetology and the basic techniques for beautifying and caring for hair, nails, and skin. At any cosmetology school, you'll

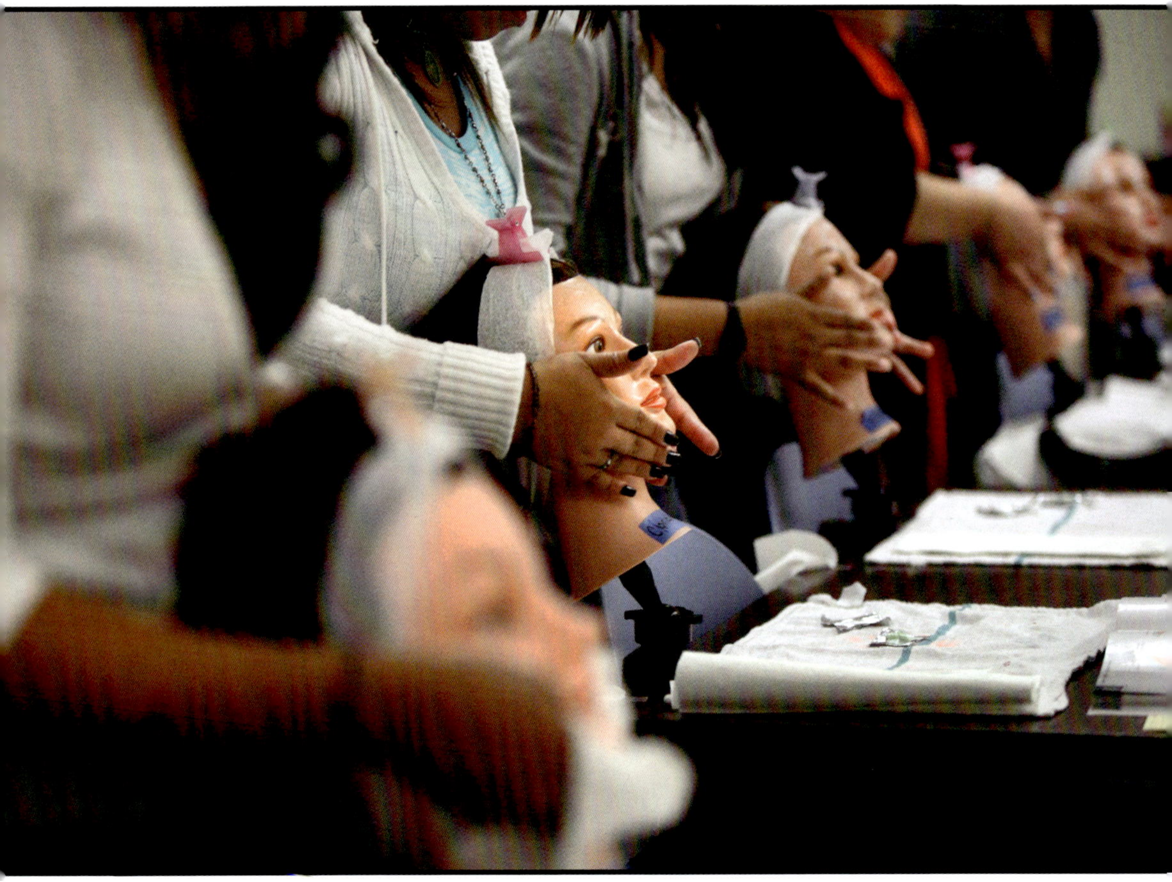

At cosmetology school, students learn the science behind cosmetology as well as numerous treatments for skin, hair, and nail care.

have a textbook to introduce basic concepts and skills. You'll take tests, just like in high school. Many beauty schools have an in-school salon for students to practice their new skills.

It might be surprising, but good cosmetologists need to know the science behind their craft. It's helpful to know the biology of how nails, skin, and hair grow and how they become damaged or diseased. Cosmetology programs also teach a bit about chemistry so that you understand how the products you use will work on your clients. It is also important to know the hazards of some of the chemicals that you will be working with as a cosmetologist.

In cosmetology school, you'll learn how to style hair like a professional, from salon shampooing techniques to strategies for sculpting every type of hair. You'll practice executing all of the classic haircuts. You'll also learn the art of hairdressing, executing hairstyles like updos and French braids. Then there are hair treatments meant to change the texture or color of hair. You'll color and dye hair, create highlights, perform permanent waves, and straighten curly hair.

In cosmetology school, you will also learn about nails. You'll give manicures and pedicures and discuss how to choose proper nail treatments. You might opt to receive some advanced training in preparing and applying acrylic nails.

And no comprehensive cosmetology education would be complete without an introduction to esthetics. In this area, you'll learn about the proper care of the skin. You'll learn how to give facials and how to safely remove unwanted body and facial hair. You'll also master makeup, from the basics to advanced techniques such as applying fake eyelashes.

Many cosmetology schools allow students to pick an area of focus. While it's important to get a strong overall education in cosmetology, it's also important to know your strengths and pursue a specialty.

HOW LONG WILL IT TAKE, AND HOW MUCH WILL IT COST?

There is no hard-and-fast answer as to how long your education will take and how much it will cost. First of all, it depends on what you want to do and where you live. If you live in Arizona and want to become an esthetician, you will need to complete 600 hours of training and practice. You can get your license in that area alone. However, if you want to be licensed as a full cosmetologist, you will need 1,600 hours of experience in order to get your license.

In New York, a cosmetologist needs 1,000 hours of training. In Idaho, 2,000 hours of training or 4,000 hours of apprenticeship are required for a cosmetology license. Of course, the process of going through cosmetology school will be longer in a state where the licensing rules require more practice hours. And if the schooling is longer, it will likely be more expensive. The average cosmetology program in the United States takes fewer than 2,000 hours to complete.

You and Sundry: A Pop-Up Salon for the Queer Community

The cosmetology industry can be very gendered. Most salons cater to women and are highly feminine spaces, while barbershops are geared to men and are hypermasculine. This can make getting a haircut an uncomfortable or intimidating experience for queer and nonbinary people. That's why Kim Goulbourne came up with the idea for You and Sundry, a pop-up hair salon that caters to women and the LGBTQIA+ community and focuses on short haircuts.

It bills itself as "a safe space where anyone can get their haircut, no matter their gender identity or expression."

"Going to get a haircut can be such an intimate experience," Goulbourne said in an interview with Racked, "and some people will refuse to get a haircut just because they don't want to tolerate ignorance or harassment. Being part of the LGBTQ+ community [and] already knowing most places may not be safe to be yourself immediately triggers discomfort."

One You and Sundry client told Racked about how uncomfortable she felt in barbershops as a queer woman. "Where other male-presenting clients were welcomed with a 'Hey boss! How are you? We'll be right with you,' I was greeted with, 'Can we help you?' as if there are other reasons to walk into a barbershop." This is why she was so relieved to discover You and Sundry. "It was a huge

(continued on the next page)

(continued from the previous page)

weight off my chest. I'd realized I'd never expressed those feelings to anyone, somehow thinking that I was the root of the problem."

You and Sundry is different from other queer hairdressing spots: it has sliding-scale prices to make it affordable to most people. Goulbourne is hoping to make You and Sundry a permanent store instead of just a pop-up in the near future.

CHOOSING THE RIGHT SCHOOL

So you've decided to take the plunge and go to cosmetology school. How do you know if you're choosing the right school?

First, consider location. Where do you want to study cosmetology? If you want to stay close to home, it makes sense to look for a beauty school nearby. However, many aspiring cosmetologists are willing to travel far from home in order to attend a quality school or study in an area of the country with lots of job opportunities.

Of course, finding a school in the right place isn't enough. You'll need to do more research, asking many questions about each program. What classes does the school offer? Do the students practice on mannequin heads, or can they practice on real clients in an in-school salon? Does the school offer the opportunity to take advanced courses in your preferred field of study?

What are the school's hours? If the school offers night and weekend classes, it may make it easier to practice

Attending beauty school gives students a chance to learn about different areas of cosmetology and discover which type of work most appeals to them.

with real, live clients or work while you go to school. How long is the program? Do students have to attend full-time, or can they go to school part-time?

It is also a good idea to find out how successful the school is at transitioning students into the working world. Does the school offer assistance with job placement after school? What percentage of the school's graduates find work in their fields?

Many students feel that it is important to go to an accredited beauty school. If a cosmetology school is accredited, it can give government financial aid to its students.

To answer these questions, read the school's materials and ask questions of school representatives. Visiting the campus can help you decide whether the school is right for you. When you're on campus, you can see the teaching style of the instructors and watch how the students interact with each other. Do you feel comfortable at the school? Do you feel inspired? Try talking to current students. What do they see as the school's strong and weak points? Contacting graduates of the program for information is a good idea, too.

BEYOND SCHOOL

Your journey to becoming a cosmetologist does not end when you finish school. Before you become a professional, you must obtain your license. You will take a written test and demonstrate your skills by carrying out a number of common beauty procedures while an examiner watches you work. Your beauty school should help you prepare for your state licensing exam.

Chapter 2

HAIRDRESSERS AND BARBERS

Many cosmetology students make the decision to go to beauty school because they want to become hairdressers, also known as hairstylists. As a hairdresser, you might work in a small-town Supercuts salon giving basic cuts to local families or in a high-fashion urban salon where stylists make big money working with demanding, wealthy clients.

Not all men feel comfortable going to a hairdresser. Some men prefer to go to a barbershop. A barber is a professional trained to cut and trim men's hair and care for their facial hair through shaves, trims, and grooming. In fact, many barbers go to special barbering schools.

Hairdressing is perhaps the most demanding and difficult of the subjects in cosmetology school. From the science of how hair grows to the ability to explain to a customer why a particular style does or doesn't work, there's a lot to learn.

THE SCIENCE OF HAIR

Good hairdressers need to understand the science of hair. During your cosmetology training, you will learn all about the anatomy of the hair. You'll study the natural life cycle of hair—how hair grows and how it stops growing, falls out, and is replaced by new hair. You will discover what makes straight hair lie flat and curly hair curl. This might sound academic—until you consider that as a hairdresser, you will often be asked to put volume and curl into straight, fine hair

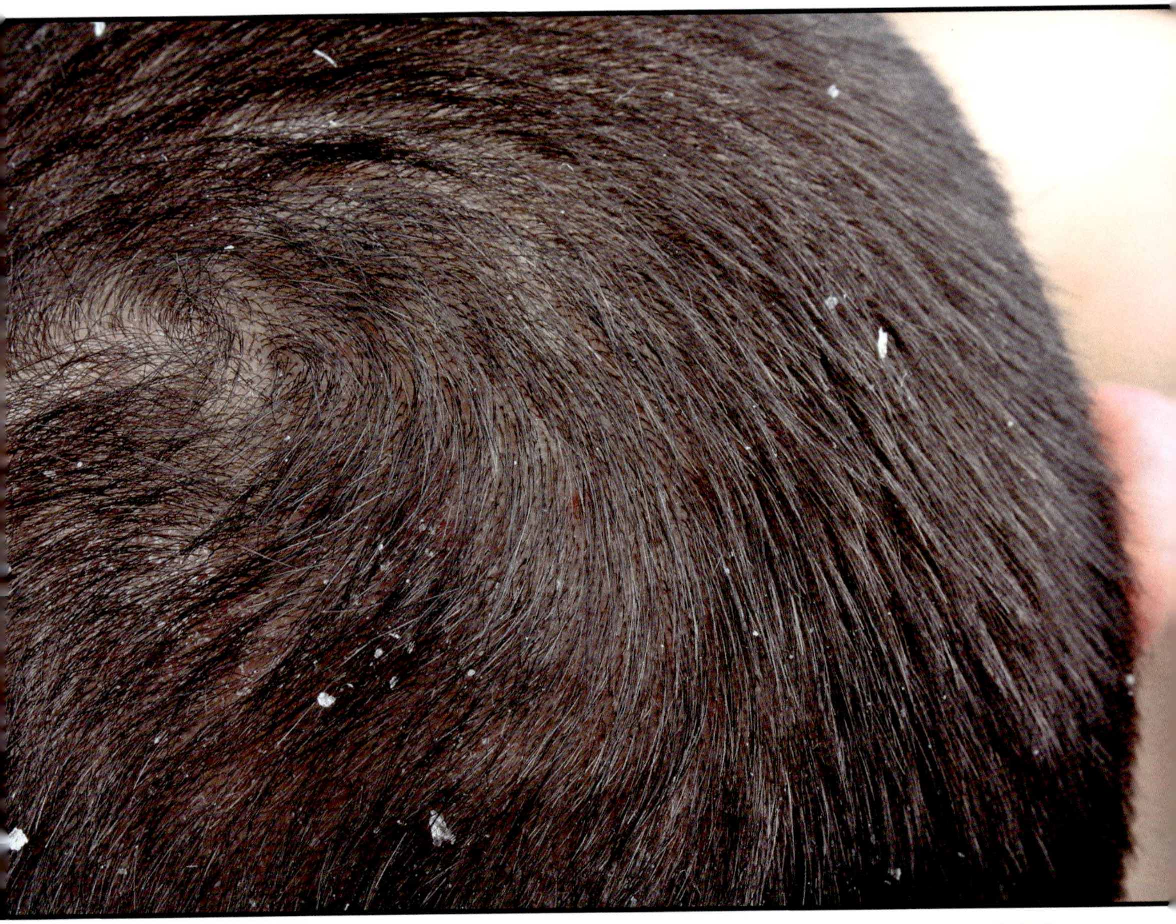

Hairdressers need to be able to identify medical conditions, such as dandruff and psoriasis, as well as pests and diseases, such as head lice and scabies.

or to make curly locks sit perfectly flat. You will likely get a basic grounding in chemistry so that you can recognize which commonly used hairdressing chemicals are useful for treating hair problems or achieving certain styling results. You will also be trained to spot medical conditions, such as dandruff and psoriasis, as well as infectious diseases and pests, such as head lice and scabies.

Your new scientific knowledge will help you answer clients' questions. It will help you plan your haircuts to look better even as they "grow out." And it will allow you to design cuts to cover bald patches, disguise thinning hair, or avoid strange growth patterns like cowlicks.

Since you'll be touching clients' scalps all day, cutting their hair, and perhaps sometimes even nicking their skin, you will learn to maintain a professional standard of hygiene. Your beauty school should teach you to disinfect your tools (scissors, brushes, combs, clips, etc.) and your work area after each client. It should emphasize the importance of keeping capes and towels freshly laundered. If you fail to maintain a high standard of cleanliness, you will run the risk of spreading infectious diseases.

HAIR CARE

Cosmetology school will introduce you to the basics of hair care for different hair types, from fine to thick, from straight to curly, from oily to dry. You'll learn which products can balance out an oily scalp, moisturize dry hair, and strengthen damaged hair.

Cosmetologists perform hair care tasks differently than untrained people do at home. There's a professional way to perform a shampoo in order to relax the hair, get rid of any tangles, massage the scalp, and prepare the entire head for a cut. There's a professional way to comb, brush, blow-dry, curl, and flat iron. These professional techniques all have one aim: to make hair look great without damaging it.

Speaking of damage, you will also learn how to spot hair that's been damaged by too much sun, clumsy or hasty styling, or excessive treatment. It's very important that you recognize damaged hair so that you can treat it gently as you cut and style it and teach the client to prevent further damage.

HAIR DESIGN

All great haircuts start with a great design. Studying hair design can help you plan your haircuts to complement different facial shapes, balance facial features, and help clients mask imperfections. For instance, oblong faces can be softened with short haircuts that kick out, or with layered looks. If a client has a round face, you can lengthen it with long hair. You'll learn what types of cuts work best for thick hair, fine hair, limp hair, tightly curled hair, and everything in between. Once you know the theory behind which cuts look great on which faces, you can customize your cuts for the lucky person sitting in your salon chair. You can start to approach your work not just as a hairdresser, but also as an artist.

HAIR CUTTING AND STYLING

Taking a full head of hair and cutting it into a new shape may sound like a daunting task. That's why you'll learn

Hairdressers need to learn the basics before they can master complicated styles and techniques. They also need to be able to work with the whole range of hair types.

how to use facial features as guides to keep your haircut symmetrical and balanced. You'll practice sectioning the hair before you cut it. And you will discover strategies for dealing with surprising hair growth patterns such as bald spots and cowlicks.

After you're trained to execute simple hairstyles like classic bobs, you'll learn advanced cutting techniques like notching, slicing, thinning, and chunking to create trendy and complicated, sometimes asymmetrical, styles. Your finishing touches are the key to creating sleek, sharp cuts; soft, feathery looks; and even chunky and funky styles.

Bias in the Beauty Industry: Caring for Ethnic and Curly Hair

Traditional cosmetology school curricula focus mostly on teaching students how to treat and care for straight hair, but many schools do not provide an adequate education in treating and caring for ethnic or curly hair. In a blog post titled "What Cosmetology School Did Not Teach Me About My Black Hair," beautician and beauty blogger Tyra Robinson describes a frustrating experience she had in beauty school. As one of only two black students in the class, Robinson ended up having to teach the whole class—and the teacher!—a lesson about how to handle black hair when she had to explain why she couldn't use shampoo on her hair.

According to a 2018 article in PuffCuff, only nineteen states require formal training in natural ethnic hair styling techniques such as braiding, twisting, and locking. "Stylists that want to cater to textured hair clients have to invest in continued education after cosmetology school for specialized training." This focus on straight hair seems to reinforce the biased cultural beauty standards that favor straight hair over curly or ethnic hair. As the author points out, "Curly and textured hair Americans spend the most money on hair care but have the least amount of options."

When considering which beauty school to apply to, it's a good idea to look for institutions that will provide you with a well-rounded education, allowing you to fully serve all your future clients. That means seeking out schools that offer programs in treatment and care for all types of ethnic and textured hair.

No visit to the hairdresser would be complete without styling. Clients need the personalized attention of the stylist so that they can see the full potential of their new look. You'll become a master stylist, using a hair dryer and brush to create volume or tame unruly and wild hair. You'll use irons to create curls or erase them. You'll be able to confidently pick styling products to recommend to customers so that they can recreate their new look at home.

Also covered in the curriculum of most beauty schools are braiding and adding extensions to your clients' hair. You may also learn how to care for wigs—a useful skill if you'd like to work in movies, television, or theater.

HAIR COLORING

Many clients visit a salon because they want to change their hair color. They might want to cover up gray hair. They might want to correct for color changes that happened after a salon disaster, overtreatment, or other damage. Or perhaps they simply want to experiment with a new look.

One of the hardest skills a hairdresser has to learn is coloring clients' hair. It's important to think carefully about the client's skin tone and natural hair color before applying a new color.

You'll learn about how to recognize clients' true hair color and respect and work with the natural coloring of their skin. You'll understand the differences among various hair shades and hair tones. You'll study how to mix colors and identify how long each color takes to "develop" once it's applied to the hair. You will practice a variety of methods for applying color to a client's hair. By the end of beauty school, you should know how to tint hair, highlight it, lowlight it, or change its color completely.

HAIR TEXTURING

Many clients book a salon appointment because they're dissatisfied with the texture of their hair. Changing a client's hair texture is one of the more difficult tasks that a hairdresser has to face.

Cosmetology school will teach you how to perform a permanent wave, or "perm," to change a client's hair from straight to curly. The process includes treating the client's hair with chemicals and heat. You'll also be initiated into the secrets of relaxing curly hair and making it straight. You may even study specialized treatments, learning to give your clients Brazilian blowouts or Japanese thermal hair straightening. Finally, you will practice instructing clients on how to care for their new style so that it will last a long time.

SPECIALISTS

If you're particularly interested in hair color or texture, you may decide to specialize in one of those areas. A salon might have a hair texture specialist who is responsible for taking on challenging texture jobs and staying informed about the latest hair texture procedures, techniques, and products. This specialist may also train other hairdressers in the salon to use new texture processes and products. Salons sometimes employ a hair color specialist, whose job is to perform expert highlights, lowlights, tints, and dye jobs. This colorist might also train fellow hairdressers in color application.

Chapter 3

ESTHETICIANS: SKIN CARE AND MAKEUP

Estheticians are experts in the maintenance and beautification of skin. They are often employed by spas or salons to give clients facials, perform body wraps, and design skin care regimens. Estheticians may also remove unwanted facial and body hair for clients. Some are trained in high-tech hair removal techniques, such as electrolysis, laser hair removal, or sugaring and threading. A firm grounding in cosmetology is recommended, as the estheticians at some spas and salons are asked to give manicures and pedicures as well.

Esthetics is a fast-growing industry and there's a lot to learn. Scientists and cosmetologists are constantly working together to create new cutting-edge techniques to rejuvenate and beautify the skin. Estheticians may also receive special training that qualifies them to offer their clients special services, such as aromatherapy, reflexology, acupuncture, LED light therapy, hydrotherapy, and acupressure. As an esthetician, there will always be something new to learn to offer more value to your clients.

The terms "esthetician" and "aesthetician" are sometimes used interchangeably to refer to people who work in salons and spas. Medical aestheticians, though, work in medical settings.

THE SCIENCE OF SKIN

You may have heard of collagen, pores, and UV rays. You probably know that each of these terms is related in some way to the skin. But could you define them all? The esthetics curriculum begins with the study of the anatomy of skin.

The hair and nails are outgrowths of the skin. Hair and nails, however, consist of dead cells. Skin, in contrast, is living. Therefore, the skin can give us an important overall indication of a person's health. When people drink enough water, eat a balanced diet, exercise, and generally take care of themselves, their skin usually looks good. If they don't get enough sleep, are constantly dehydrated, or overindulge in alcohol, cigarettes, or drugs, this tends to take a toll on their skin. Unhealthy living ages the skin prematurely. A good esthetician also learns to recognize various skin disorders. If you treat someone with a serious skin condition inappropriately, you may harm that person. Moreover, if you treat a client with an infectious skin disease, you could spread that disease to other clients—

Estheticians work with the skin. Esthetics is a fast-growing industry, with more and more people choosing to get facials and other skin treatments on a regular basis.

or even catch it yourself. Not every disease is visible to the eye. That's why it's important that every esthetician maintain a sanitary, sterile work environment.

FACIALS AND OTHER SKIN TREATMENTS

One of the most satisfying and creative parts of being an esthetician is giving facial treatments. A facial typically includes removing the client's makeup, cleansing and toning the skin, and perhaps applying eye cream, massage cream, or other products. The esthetician might also

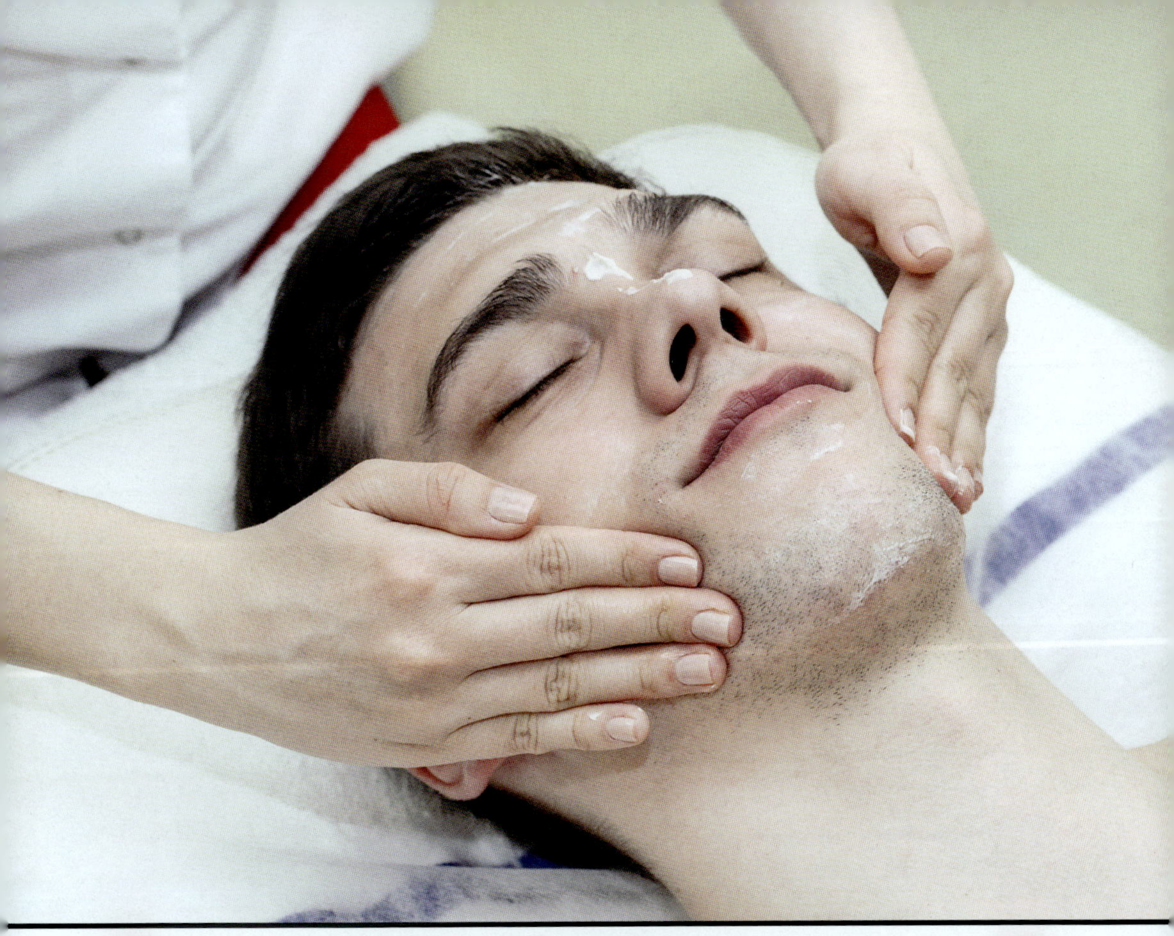

Some facial treatments involve applying a mask to replenish the skin and exfoliating scrubs to get rid of the dead skin cells on the top layer of the skin.

massage the face, scalp, and shoulders to stimulate blood circulation.

Other parts of a facial will vary from client to client. Exfoliating scrubs help clear away the very top layer of the skin, which is generally made up of dead cells, and reveal the healthy, vital cells beneath. This is also the goal of facial treatments such as microdermabrasion. In microdermabrasion, the esthetician uses a special machine to blast dead cells off the surface of the face and reveal the younger, glowing skin underneath.

Fauzia Morgan: Pro Tips from an Esthetician

Fauzia Morgan is a licensed esthetician who runs a successful skin therapy business. Her interest in skin care grew out of her personal experience of learning to address her own acne through acupuncture and dietary changes, learning to "heal her body from the inside out." In a previous job at a pharmacy, she realized she could help people with their own skin issues by recommending natural products and referring them to acupuncturists and naturopaths. Then, when she decided to go to esthetician school, she chose a school that "emphasized the whole body and the ways in which internal health affects the skin."

In a profile in NaturalHealers.com, Morgan encourages aspiring estheticians to spend lots of time networking. "Sharing space and clients with other professionals can be a great way to build your business." She also emphasizes the importance of sincerity. "I can only sell something I believe in 100 percent.... People trust me because I'm passionate about the products and I know them well." Professionals should also keep learning and building their skills. Since many skin care lines offer courses to the professionals who use their products, take advantage of these opportunities to make sure you truly know the products you're working with.

Morgan's final piece of advice is to remember self-care. "Taking care of yourself is so important when you're in a

field where you take care of other people." She suggests doing something to relax in between clients, such as taking a walk or stretching, as well as maintaining a healthy lifestyle with plenty of exercise. "People are coming to you for a peaceful experience and for their monthly or bimonthly treat. You have to be in a good mental, physical, and emotional space."

The esthetician may also add a facial steam, pack, or mask. In your cosmetology program, you'll learn how to choose a prepared mask or design and create your own facial mask out of pure ingredients. The point of a facial mask—whether it is made from cucumbers, yogurt, honey, or mud—is to replenish and balance the skin. The same is true for packs, cream masks, and gel masks.

There are so many treatments, techniques, and options for people hoping to improve their skin. The choices are positively dizzying. That's why clients are willing to pay to consult with a skin care professional who can help them craft a personalized skin care plan.

PARAMEDICAL AESTHETICIANS

Paramedical aestheticians work in doctors' offices, helping to prepare clients for cosmetic surgery and other medical procedures. Paramedical aestheticians might offer other services like Botox injections, chemical peels, skin care after surgery, and hair removal for clients whose medical situation disqualifies them from seeing a regular aesthetician. Paramedical aestheticians also offer clients preoperative and postoperative care for face-lifts. They might also use makeup to help clients conceal healing skin while recovering from surgery. In many states, paramedical aestheticians need a special license.

WAXING AND OTHER HAIR REMOVAL TECHNIQUES

Skin care is not the only area that estheticians handle. Estheticians are often tasked with hair removal through waxing, plucking, or more specialized techniques. Any hair removal process starts with a client consultation. Some clients should not undergo hair removal. If they have certain allergies, skin disorders, or are taking certain medications, having hair professionally removed may be dangerous to their health.

Estheticians learn how to remove body and facial hair from both men and women. This might be a simple procedure, such as an eyebrow wax. It could involve using tweezers to pluck and shape certain areas or using a depilatory to weaken the hair and make it easier to remove. Whatever the method, you will have to learn to perform the hair removal procedure in the cleanest, most efficient, and least painful way possible. A waxer or other esthetician who can be trusted to keep clean conditions and treat clients with compassion will likely win a lot of return business.

Estheticians may also learn more advanced forms of hair removal. These tend to be more expensive than waxing and tweezing, but they last longer, are cleaner, and in some cases, lead to permanent hair removal. These other methods of hair removal require advanced training and sometimes a separate license.

Electrolysis is a popular method of permanent hair removal. This method may sound somewhat strange. The esthetician slides an extremely thin metal probe into a hair follicle and zaps it with electricity. The hair is destroyed, and the hope is that after several treatments, the hair follicle will be permanently damaged and will no longer produce hairs. There are many methods of electrolysis, all using different equipment. As an advanced procedure, electrolysis requires its own training. In many states, electrologists must obtain their own special licenses.

Laser hair removal works along the same lines as electrolysis. Instead of inserting metal rods into the hair follicle, the hair follicle is damaged with a laser. Another related hair removal process is photoepilation, which involves intense pulsed light.

OTHER ESTHETIC METHODS AND TREATMENTS

Esthetics professionals are constantly at work inventing new ways to rejuvenate and beautify skin. The following are a few of the advanced methods that you may offer your clients as an esthetician:

Desincrustation uses a weak but steady electrical current to increase the amount of fluid that the skin can absorb and then flushes the skin with fluid. It is good for making oily skin less greasy and hydrating dry skin.

Manual lymphatic draining is a type of massage that keeps lymph flowing through the body's lymphatic system, which helps immunize the body against disease. This massage is supposed to help the lymphatic system purge excess bacteria and waste.

Microcurrent uses low doses of electrical current to imitate the electrical signals that cells send when the body is healing. This electricity is supposed to jump-start the body's healing process. Estheticians use it to fight the effects of aging on the skin.

Acupressure is a type of massage that stimulates pressure points (similar to those used in acupuncture) to relieve pain and stimulate healing.

Aromatherapy uses fragrant oils and other fragranced products to reduce stress and promote a better mood. Some aromatherapists claim that aromatherapy can also be used to treat illness.

Hydrotherapy uses water to relieve pain, relax patients, and sometimes treat specific medical problems. Hydrotherapy is practiced in many spas and can take many different forms, including mineral baths, underwater massage, or even a simple soak in a hot tub.

LED light therapy uses light waves that can pass through the skin to encourage damaged cells to heal. Estheticians use this therapy to treat acne and reduce wrinkles.

MAKEUP ARTISTS

Part of your comprehensive cosmetology education will be learning about makeup. You'll begin by learning cosmetic color theory—what colors pair well with various skin tones and hair colors. You'll be trained to use all the

Some cosmetologists become professional makeup artists. If you are particularly interested in makeup, you may decide to go to a makeup academy.

major forms of cosmetics, from everyday items like lipstick and lip gloss to complicated cosmetics like individual fake eyelashes. Above all, cosmetology school will teach you how to use makeup to emphasize striking features, while downplaying features the client dislikes. This is called corrective makeup.

Learning about makeup is typically a small part of cosmetology school, but there are people who make a living solely as makeup artists. There are even makeup academies where you can focus on specialty makeup, such as fashion makeup, bridal makeup, and special effects makeup.

Some makeup artists make a living simply by working in cosmetic stores, beauty supply stores, or at cosmetic counters in department stores. There is no special training needed for these jobs. In fact, some beauty professionals recommend that if you are considering a career as a makeup artist, you might want to first get a job at a makeup counter or makeup store. That way, you can see whether the field is truly to your liking before investing in beauty school or makeup school.

As technology makes it easier to document people's lives, makeup artists are more in demand than ever to prepare ordinary people for special events like weddings and proms. Bridal makeup is a lucrative and growing field. Even funeral homes employ makeup artists for mortuary makeup. At higher levels, skilled makeup artists are in demand to prepare models for fashion shoots and runway shows. You must be extremely well respected and lucky to land these jobs.

Of course, theater, film, and television productions always need makeup artists. The work in these industries can range from simply making a great-looking star look even better to artificially aging a young person, changing a person's gender, or even creating an outlandish character like an orc, werewolf, dwarf, or alien. Special-effects makeup is extremely specialized and uses all sorts of advanced techniques like airbrushing and latex application. Some special-effects makeup artists attend special schools, while others apprentice with an established special-effects makeup artist.

PERMANENT MAKEUP

"Permanent makeup" refers to the practice of tattooing designs that imitate makeup onto a client—for instance, applying lines on the eyelids that look like eyeliner or eye shadow. This field combines the skills of the makeup artist and the tattoo artist. The job is high stakes, and there is very little room for error. It requires special training and licensing. The demand for these services varies greatly from region to region. Research the demand for permanent-makeup artists in your area before you commit to a course of study.

Chapter 4

MANICURISTS AND NAIL TECHNICIANS

In cosmetology school, in addition to learning about hair and skin, you'll spend time learning about nails. You may even decide to make nails the focus of your career and become a manicurist, also known as a nail technician. Nail technicians are trained to clean, trim, and polish fingernails and toenails. Many enhance their clients' experiences by providing hand, arm, foot, and leg massages.

At more advanced levels, manicurists may lengthen clients' nails using acrylic or gel nails. Some nail techs work in nail salons, which concentrate exclusively on giving manicures and pedicures. Others work in salons and spas that offer a wider array of services. In some salons, the manicurist may offer hair removal services or double as an esthetician. Still other manicurists work toward opening their own nail shop.

A comprehensive cosmetology education will definitely come in handy as a nail technician because at some salons, manicurists are also expected to provide hair removal services.

THE SCIENCE OF NAILS

Before you beautify a person's body, you must understand it from the inside out. Manicurists or nail technicians must understand the anatomy of nails. They need to know how nails grow, what makes them weak, what makes them break, and what strengthens them. They should understand the chemistry of the nail so that they will know why certain substances adhere to the nails. This is especially important for nail technicians since they spend so much time painting nails, coating them, or stripping them.

SAFETY AND HYGIENE

Just as in other areas of cosmetology, it's important to learn about safety and hygiene when working with nails. Some clients may be allergic to your materials, from nail primers and polishes to gel or acrylic tips. Nail techs work with a wide array of chemicals and processes that need to be treated with care. It is important, for instance, to the health of nail technicians and clients that manicures and pedicures be performed in well-ventilated areas.

Nail technicians should also know how to spot and deal with common problems, such as the fungal infections that can sometimes develop in the space between a natural nail and the false nail laid down on top of it.

Nail technicians are trained in the art and science of nail care. They start out by learning about the anatomy of nails before moving on to learning various manicure techniques.

MANICURES AND PEDICURES

As a nail tech, you'll become an expert at performing manicures and pedicures. Typically, the nail technician follows a number of steps, including exfoliation and moisturizing; trimming or pushing back the cuticles;

shaping, buffing, and cleaning the nails; and finally, polishing and drying. The manicure may include extra services, such as a paraffin wax dip or a massage. Nail technicians also learn to do specialized manicures, such as men's manicures.

Pedicures follow the same basic procedure as manicures but come with their own set of challenges and rewards. If you're a person who hates looking at and touching feet, becoming a nail tech is definitely not for you! Not only will you have to clean and shape toenails, you will also have to file off calluses and deal with corns and blisters.

During cosmetology training, you'll learn how to create different edges on nails using files, emery boards, cuticle knives, electric files, and other tools. You'll learn about how different shapes may complement or detract from various hand shapes—and what kinds of manicures will work best for different clients. Just as a wild haircut will detract from a conservative client's life, an easily broken manicure will be totally inappropriate for a client who works with her hands.

NAIL ART AND DESIGN

The fun part of giving manicures and pedicures is the ability to transform a client's nails through polish or nail art. Some of the nail designs covered in cosmetology programs include full coverage, half moon, hairline, and free edge. In cosmetology school, you will practice giving manicures that are designed to simply augment and perfect the natural look of a hand, as well as manicures that involve acrylic tips and outlandish colors.

Many people love to express themselves with nail art and extensions. There are so many options for nail care, including silk wraps, acrylic tips, and gel nails.

Today, there are so many ways for clients to make a fashion statement with their nails. Many manicurists enjoy creating fun nail designs or using nail wraps that allow them to apply complex pictures and patterns to nails, much like pasting over a billboard.

ARTIFICIAL NAILS AND NAIL ENHANCEMENTS

Many people go to cosmetology school to learn how to do the demanding work of creating nail tips and extensions. These "fake nails" are much more complicated and demanding than press-ons. As a nail technician, your clients will look to you to create strong, natural-looking, and fashionable nails. Some of the nail extension technologies that you might be called upon to use include silk, fiberglass, or linen wraps; acrylic tips; and gel nails.

Wraps are used to add strength and length to the nail. This can be done with silk, which is flexible, lightweight, and natural; linen, which is strong and thick and can be more noticeable than silk; and fiberglass, which can be both strong and flexible. These wraps are especially useful if the natural nail underneath a tip or extension has been damaged and must be protected.

Nail technicians also use acrylic nails to add length. First, artificial tips are added onto the nail. Next, the nail and tip together are covered with a layer of acrylic. A perfect shape is achieved by fitting a form over the nail and tip. After about fifteen minutes, the nails harden. These nails are formed chemically, so they must be removed with solvents.

Part of a manicurist's job includes applying nail extensions. These "fake nails" are hard to create because they must be strong and look good.

Gel nails are similar in many ways to acrylic nails. Gel nails can look very natural, and they do not need to be polished to look great. They harden under a UV light. Plus, while acrylic nails have a strong odor, gel nails have the advantage of being almost odorless. However, gel nails are very difficult to remove; basically, the client must grow his or her nails out and cut the gel off a bit at a time.

Both acrylic and gel nails need to be filled regularly. As the natural nail grows out, it pushes the artificial nail away from the cuticle, leaving a gap between the skin

Massage Therapists

Massage therapists are often employed by a salon or spa to give clients relaxing and rejuvenating massages as part of a luxurious spa experience. But massage therapists can also alleviate serious physical pain. Using touch, physical pressure, and manipulations of the muscles through the skin, massage therapists can significantly improve a client's life.

If you're interested in a career as a massage therapist, forgo cosmetology school and proceed directly to massage school. You'll learn many different techniques, including deep tissue massage, Swedish massage, Japanese shiatsu massage, and sports massage. Massage therapists may find employment with a salon, spa, hotel, resort, retirement home, or even a sports team. Others are self-employed, traveling with portable massage tables and making their own schedules.

and the artificial nail. A nail technician can "fill in" the gap with more gel or acrylic. This will also keep the nail strong. Nail technicians also need to make sure that their clients understand how to care for their artificial nails properly.

NAIL TECHNOLOGY SCHOOL

Many students who know that they want to focus exclusively on nail technology may decide to skip cosmetology or beauty school and go straight to nail technology school.

It is possible to obtain a license to do nails only, and the amount of time required to get this license is much shorter than the overall cosmetologist degree or license sequence. However, nail techs who exclusively give manicures and pedicures tend to make less money than cosmetologists who are able to offer their clients services in several different areas. Therefore, if you decide to go to nail technology school, you should be completely sure that nail care is what you want to focus on.

Chapter 5

MANAGERS AND BUSINESS OWNERS

Once you've been working in a salon or spa for a while, you may be looking for opportunities to move up the ladder or branch out on your own. Many cosmetologists go on to become managers or even open their own businesses. Running or owning your own business certainly comes with additional challenges, but with the increased responsibility comes more freedom and usually more money as well.

SALON MANAGERS

A busy salon needs a manager to keep the establishment running in an efficient and professional manner. The manager's job is to hire, train, and schedule employees.

Many cosmetologists dream of one day opening their own salon or spa. If you choose this route, make sure you have a strong vision for how your salon will stand out from the competition.

He or she also hires receptionists, janitors, and other staff. Managers order beauty supplies and ensure that the salon's equipment is in working order. Above all, the salon manager sees that the salon is running smoothly and that customers are happy.

Managing a salon isn't a job that you get straight out of beauty school. In general, managers start out as hair stylists or estheticians. They learn about the creative side of the trade, get a little experience, and see how the salon works. After that, they may be able to take on more managerial responsibility.

Running a salon comes with a great deal of responsibilities, including making sure the salon is supplied with all the products that may be needed on any given day.

SALON OR SPA OWNERS

Ambitious individuals with a passion for beauty often dream of owning their own salon or spa. The routes to this career are numerous. You might buy an existing salon so that you don't need to choose a location, buy fixtures, or build a clientele. Or you might build an entirely new salon from the ground up.

As the owner of a salon or spa, you must be aware of every detail of the business. Before attempting to be an owner, you should have already mastered all of the skills of the salon manager. Besides this, you must also deal with paying rent, paying employees, marketing the salon, attracting customers, and a thousand other day-to-day details of running a business. You must have a vision for your business so that you can create a plan of action that will make your dream a reality. This is a difficult career path, but the rewards can be tremendous.

Because there is so much involved in starting a successful business (or even buying an existing business and keeping it successful), many salon owners decide to study business at the college or graduate level.

BEAUTY SUPPLY STORE OWNERS

There are so many aspects of the beauty industry that take place outside of the salon. One important place is the beauty supply store, where professional cosmetologists—and some nonprofessionals—go to purchase shampoos, conditioners, cosmetics, styling tools, extensions, hair colors, and other supplies. If you've gone to beauty school, you, as the owner of a beauty supply store, will be able to apply your knowledge of basic anatomy and chemistry, your familiarity with the best brands and products, and your awareness of what tools beauty professionals need.

If your ambition is to own a beauty supply store, you may want to invest in business education. A solid business education will help you run your business in a professional manner and allow you to avoid unnecessary mistakes that could cost you your dream.

Jordan Samuel Pacitti: From Ballet Dancer to Skin Care Brand Creator

Jordan Samuel Pacitti became interested in skin care when he began having to wear heavy stage makeup as a dancer in the Pacific Northwest Ballet. "The heavy makeup I was wearing was meant to stay there and not budge. I began to get facials because my face needed deep cleansing," Pacitti told Rachel Brown in a profile in Beauty Independent.

After he retired from ballet, Pacitti went to esthetics school to pursue his interest in skin care. He worked in spas for a while and then decided to branch out on his own and launch his own skin care brand. In 2012, he opened his own small facial practice, and in 2013, he launched his own skin care brand, offering four products: cleanser, facial mist, facial serum, and facial oil.

Jordan Samuel is a direct-to-consumer brand, meaning the products are not available in stores. "If you go direct-to-consumer you can be 50 to 60 percent less in price because you don't have to have retail margins. I can make the amount of money I would be making, but the customer is paying half." This direct-to-consumer approach has proved to be a lucrative strategy. The brand grew 500 percent in 2017 and became a million-dollar brand in 2018.

COSMETOLOGY INSTRUCTORS

It takes a special sort of person to become an instructor in a cosmetology school. Good teachers are organized, confident, patient, compassionate, perceptive, and passionate. They know how to communicate ideas clearly and succinctly. Of course, instructors should have several years of real-world experience under their belts and have a good reputation in the industry. The more respected you are in your field, the more attractive you will be to schools that might want to hire you.

Some beauty schools offer teacher training. Ask your favorite teachers at your beauty school how they got to where they are today. Perhaps you will be able to emulate their career paths.

SALON TRAINERS AND MANUFACTURER EDUCATORS

Being a cosmetology instructor is just one way of working as an educator in the beauty industry. Many larger salons employ salon trainers. Salon trainers are responsible for training new employees to perform advanced techniques, such as hot new haircuts or new esthetics techniques. As a salon trainer, you will help experienced cosmetology professionals improve their skills so that they can make their clients' lives better in a number of ways.

Many beauty supply manufacturers also employ cosmetologists as manufacturer educators. Manufacturer educators travel to salons and train cosmetologists to properly use their products. For instance, a person who

There are plenty of jobs for cosmetologists in the fashion industry. It can be an exciting field to work in, but it often involves working under pressure in a fast-paced environment.

works as a manufacturer educator might travel throughout the northeastern United States introducing hairdressers to a new styling gel.

FASHION INDUSTRY JOBS

Stylists who work in prestigious salons are sometimes given the opportunity to create hairstyles for fashion magazines and runway fashion shows. While this work can be exciting, fulfilling, and creative, it can also be difficult and fast paced. In fashion shows, most stylists will work under a main stylist who creates the overall look; other stylists must learn the hairstyles and be ready to work quickly under pressure. In this industry, you need to know how to deal with people with difficult personalities, as well as how to keep cool under pressure by troubleshooting small problems quickly and creatively.

Other fashion industry jobs include writers and editors for beauty and lifestyle magazines, trade show directors, and beauty product marketers.

Chapter 6

GETTING STARTED IN YOUR CAREER

Cosmetology is a fast-growing industry, and prospects look good for those hoping to work in the field. According to 2018 data from the Bureau of Labor Statistics, jobs for barbers, hairdressers, and cosmetologists were projected to grow 13 percent, which is faster than the average rate for all occupations. This increase will be due in part to population growth and in part to the rising demand for hair coloring, straightening, and other advanced hair treatments. However, beauty is a competitive industry that can be hard to break into, so it's important to plan ahead to give yourself the best chance of landing your dream job.

APPRENTICESHIPS

Most employers prefer to hire someone with experience, but if nobody hires you, how will you gain experience? Luckily, many well-respected salons run apprenticeship programs. As an apprentice hairstylist, you will observe master hairstylists at work and assist them. You may also shampoo clients, sweep up hair, and help keep clients comfortable. The salon managers are not only concerned

An apprenticeship is a great way to start a career in the cosmetology industry. Apprentices work alongside experienced professionals and learn from them.

that you learn how to cut, color, and texture according to their methods. They also want to know that you will fit into the salon's culture—that you can be friendly and professional with clients and a good team member with your salon colleagues.

The pay for these jobs varies from place to place. In many salons, the apprentices earn minimum wage, plus any tips. You may be given the opportunity to give your own haircuts for a lower fee than senior stylists.

Although apprenticeships are often associated with hairdressing, estheticians have assistants and apprentices, too. Research the apprenticeship and internship opportunities in your area. Some savvy students become apprentices while they are still going through cosmetology school. That way, they are more likely to be ready to earn their license and go straight to work when they graduate.

Some students go on to work at the same salon where they apprentice. However, this depends on a variety of factors. Before you take an apprentice job at a salon, it's worth asking yourself how well you fit in there. Do you feel comfortable? Have friends? Could you see yourself spending the next few years working there? If you play your cards right, you may earn work experience and get your foot in the door at a great salon—before you even graduate from cosmetology school!

CAREER SERVICES AT COSMETOLOGY SCHOOL

Many cosmetology schools offer their graduates assistance with career planning and job placement. This means that the school guides you in your search and, in some cases, actively helps you find a job. In fact, this is one of the main factors you should consider when you are deciding where to go to school. Ask the schools to which you are applying for details on their job placement programs and other career services. Don't be afraid to ask to see job placement statistics or lists of graduates who have found work in prestigious salons.

JOB HUNTING

Although you may dream that after beauty school glamorous salons and spas will be immediately fighting over your services, the reality is that you will probably join many other new graduates as a job hunter. One well-known job-hunting technique is to check job listing websites and message boards for open positions. To reply to these kinds of ads, you'll need an updated, neat, and professional-looking résumé. You'll also need an impressive portfolio, or "book," with photographs of your best work to date. Choose just a few exceptional looks to showcase. The styles you include in your portfolio should give the viewer a taste of your personal style while demonstrating that you can adapt your artistic vision to meet a client's needs.

In addition to applying for advertised positions, there are other job-hunting strategies you can try. Networking is important. Let your friends know that you're in the market for a new job. Ask your friends to tell you if they know about any salons that are looking for employees. Poll your friends and family about their favorite salons and spas, then contact those places and let them know you are looking for work. Your classmates can be another good source of information—especially those who graduated

When you are looking for a job, it can be a good idea to visit local salons in person and drop off your résumé with the manager. Even if he or she is not hiring at the time, the manager may keep it on file.

before you. Consider creating a website or social media page highlighting your work, inspirations, and personal style. This can help you sell yourself to future employers.

If you are bold, try stopping by a salon or spa that you admire to show your résumé and book. Even if that establishment is not hiring, the staff might be able to tell you about a place that is. Or perhaps they'll just keep your résumé on file. Either way, introducing yourself in a friendly and professional manner can't hurt! Always keep a positive attitude.

Social Media Influencers and the Future of the Beauty Industry

The beauty industry has seen many changes over the years, and it continues to adapt with the times. With the rise of social media and direct-to-consumer marketing, anyone can now start his or her own beauty brand. Established beauty brands are having to compete with lots of new independent brands, and many of these brands are skilled at reaching consumers directly via social media. Many brands find success by getting the endorsement of YouTube celebrities and "influencers"—people who have large social media followings and a lot of influence on which products consumers choose to purchase.

Michelle Phan, a twenty-seven-year-old internet sensation based in Boston, started building a social media community in 2007, when she was still in high school, by doing makeup tutorials on YouTube. She now has twenty-seven million followers and regularly works with huge global brands. L'Oreal even partnered with Phan to create a line of makeup designed by her.

These influencers are building careers for themselves and changing the beauty industry at the same time. According to Richard Kestenbaum writing in *Forbes*, traditional makeup sales were down 1.3 percent in 2016 while independent brands' sales were up by 42.7 percent. Traditional companies have realized they need to listen to the new generation of consumers and change the way they operate.

If all else fails, you can consider getting your foot in the door at a great salon or spa by starting out in a noncreative position, such as receptionist. In the meantime, keep making yourself more attractive to employers by staying on top of the latest techniques and learning how to do the hottest new procedures.

PLANNING YOUR CAREER

It's important to develop a clear image of what you want your career to be like. If you don't know what you want out of a career in cosmetology, it's easy to drift, unsure of the best route to take. Working in a salon seems just as good as working for yourself; staying in rural Alaska seems as good as moving to New York. But if you can articulate exactly what you'd like your life to be like, you can plan backward and craft a series of action steps for yourself.

Perhaps you dream of working backstage at fashion shows as a hairstylist. This may seem like an impossible goal to reach, but the journey of a thousand miles begins with a single step. Brainstorm a series of action steps that will move you closer to your goal, bit by bit. For instance, the most important fashion shows take place during fashion weeks: periods of time when designers show their collections in cities like New York, Los Angeles, and Miami. If you want to work backstage at a fashion show, you'll need to live and work in a city that has a fashion week. The stylists backstage at fashion shows are often hairdressers who work at prestigious salons. So you'll need to get a job at a respected salon in the city.

When planning your cosmetology career, start out by thinking about your dream job, then write a list of action steps to help you achieve your goals.

Next, break each action step down into even smaller action steps. For instance, before you can get a job at a prestigious salon, you need to know which salons are prestigious. Research the hottest salons in your city, and try to meet people who work in them. (Your school's career services can be helpful in making these kinds of contacts.) Then ask your contacts at those salons what they look for in employees. Where did most of their hairstylists go to beauty school? What qualities do these salons look for in an employee?

If you can't even imagine what action steps might lead you toward your goal, get online and research some people who have already achieved your career goal. Contact them politely and respectfully, and ask them if they would be willing to talk to you about how they got to where they are. If you find people who are willing to answer some of your questions, you might want to ask: did they go to beauty school? Which one? Did they gain some valuable experience in high school? Do they have any advice for aspiring cosmetologists? Ask yourself how you might follow the career path that they forged.

You can learn more about how to fulfill your beauty industry goals by reading trade publications such as *American Salon and Modern Salon*. Consider attending beauty conventions and trade shows. Talk with any professionals you meet. Connect with cosmetologists in your area and ask them to share their thoughts about how you might build a career.

If you find yourself knocked off course, working in a job you don't love or a place you wish you could escape, don't give up. Everyone experiences career setbacks.

Keep trying to figure out how to get to where you want to be. In the meantime, keep educating yourself and improving your skills. Be prepared so that when an opportunity presents itself, you will be ready to seize it.

Launching a career may seem daunting now—and no one will tell you that it's going to be easy. But if you have a passion for beauty and you have determination, vision, and grit, eventually you will build a career. As Vidal Sassoon once said, "The only place where success comes before work is in the dictionary."

Glossary

BARBER A licensed professional who usually cuts men's hair.

COSMETOLOGY The cosmetic treatment of hair, skin, and nails.

COWLICK A lock of hair that grows in a different direction from the hair around it.

CUTICLE A part of the skin that covers and protects the edge of the fingernails.

ELECTROLYSIS A process of removing hair that involves using a direct electrical current to damage hair follicles.

ESTHETICIAN A licensed skin care professional; also known as aesthetician.

EXFOLIATION The removal of dead skin cells on the surface of the skin by mechanical or chemical means.

EXTENSIONS Human or artificial hair integrated with natural hair to make the hair longer; also known as a hair weave.

FACIAL TREATMENT A beauty treatment designed to treat, exfoliate, invigorate, and refresh the skin on the face.

LASER HAIR REMOVAL A method of hair removal that involves using lasers to damage the hair follicles.

LGBTQIA+ Lesbian, gay, bisexual, transgender, queer, intersex, and other alternative identities relating to gender or sexuality.

MANICURIST A licensed professional who grooms hands and feet and may polish nails or apply fake nails; also known as a nail technician.

NAIL TECHNICIAN A licensed professional who grooms hands and feet and may polish nails or apply fake nails; also known as a manicurist.

NOTCHING A method of cutting hair to create a chunky effect.

PERMANENT WAVE A hair treatment that makes the hair wavy and lasts until the hair grows out.

PHOTOEPILATION A method of removing hair using light; can include intense pulsed light (IPL) or laser treatment.

PSORIASIS A skin condition that can be itchy or painful.

RELAXING Chemically straightening hair.

SCABIES A skin condition caused by an infestation of mites inside the skin.

SLICING A method of cutting hair that removes bulk and adds movement.

THINNING A method of cutting thick hair to make it thinner.

For More Information

Allied Beauty Association
145 Traders Boulevard East, Units 26 & 27
Mississauga, ON L4Z 3L3
Canada
(800) 268-6644
Website: https://www.abacanada.com
Facebook, Instagram, and Twitter: @ABAcanada
A Canadian nonprofit member association representing professionals in the beauty industry. It offers resources, a job board, and regular events.

American Association of Cosmetology Schools (AACS)
9927 East Bell Road, Suite 110
Scottsdale, AZ 85260
(800) 831-1086
Website: http://beautyschools.org
Facebook: @AmericanAssociationofCosmetologySchools
Twitter: @AACSchools
AACS is a membership organization of professionals in cosmetology, barbering, and massage. It offers seminars, conferences, conventions, and advocacy.

Beauty Council
203-8047 199 Street
Langly, BC V2Y 0E2
Canada
(604) 871-0222
Website: https://www.beautycouncil.ca
Facebook: @beautycouncilwesterncanada
Instagram and Twitter: @BeautyCouncil

Beauty Council is a professional membership organization serving the beauty industry in western Canada. It offers classes and nationally recognized certification for cosmetologists.

Beauty Schools Directory
(844) 528-8612
Website: https://www.beautyschoolsdirectory.com
Facebook and Instagram: @beautyschoolsdirectory
Twitter: @BeautySchoolsD
The Beauty Schools Directory is an online resource with a comprehensive list of cosmetology schools across the country, searchable by location.

National Association of Barber Boards of America (NABBA)
3336 Cypresswood Drive South
Jacksonville, FL 32257
(888) 338-0101
Website: https://www.nationalbarberboards.com
NABBA is a membership association for professionals in the barbering industry, dedicated to maintaining professional standards in the industry. It hosts an annual conference.

National-Interstate Council of State Boards of Cosmetology (NIC)
7622 Briarwood Circle
Little Rock, AR 72205
(501) 277-8262
Website: https://nictesting.org

NIC offers nationally recognized certification as well as resources and practice tests for students and professionals in the cosmetology industry.

Professional Beauty Association (PBA)
15825 North 71st Street, #100
Scottsdale, AZ 85254
(800) 468-2274
Website: https://probeauty.org
Facebook: @professionalbeautyassociation
Twitter and Instagram: @ProBeautyAssoc
PBA is a membership organization for cosmetologists offering advocacy, education, events, and resources.

For Further Reading

Grissler, Jeff. *How to Get a J.O.B in a Salon: Cosmetology School Graduate 3*. Fort Collins, CO: Ready, Set, Go Publishing, 2013.

Heos, Bridget. *Getting a Job in Hair Care and Makeup*. New York, NY: Rosen Publishing, 2014.

Herzner, Carrie. *The Business of Beauty: Your Guide to Happiness and Success in the Salon Industry*. Cincinnati, OH: Goat Tree Press, 2014.

Institute for Career Research. *Careers in Cosmetology: Beautician*. Chicago, IL: Institute for Career Research, 2015.

Marlow, Christie. *Cosmetologist*. Bromall, PA: Mason Crest, 2014.

Newman, Marian. *The Complete Nail Technician*. Boston, MA: Cengage Learning, 2017.

Nixon, James, and Bobby Humphrey. *Hairdresser*. London, UK: Franklin Watts, 2014.

Paige, Danielle. *How to Become a Beauty Therapist: The Complete Insider's Guide to Becoming a Beauty Therapist*. How 2 Become Ltd., 2015.

Royston, Angela. *Skin Deep: The Business of Beauty.* London, UK: Franklin Watts, 2015.

Sandlin, Eileen Figure. *Start Your Own Hair Salon and Day Spa: Your Step-by-Step Guide to Success*. Irvine, CA: Entrepreneur Press, 2014.

Bibliography

Allied Beauty Association. "What Is the ABA?" Retrieved November 12, 2018. https://www.abacanada.com/shows1-1.

American Association of Cosmetology Schools. "Careers in Beauty." Retrieved October 1, 2018. http://beautyschools.org/careers-in-beauty.

Ancient Pages. "Nail Polish Was Used in 3000 B.C. –Color of Fingernails Indicated Social Status in Ancient China and Egypt." January 11, 2018. http://www.ancientpages.com/2018/01/11/nail-polish-was-used-in-3000-b-c-color-of-fingernails-indicated-social-status-in-ancient-china-and-egypt.

Aveda Institute. "Ten Outside-the-Box Jobs You Can Pursue with a Cosmetology License." Retrieved October 1, 2018. https://douglasj.edu/ten-outside-the-box-jobs-you-can-pursue-with-a-cosmetology-license.

Bailly, Jenny. "O Investigation: Hair Straightening Treatments." Oprah. Retrieved November 12, 2018. https://www.oprah.com/style/the-truth-about-hair-straightening-treatments.

Baniamor. "Navigating the Intensely Gendered World of Hair Salons When You're Queer." Racked, August 23, 2018. https://www.racked.com/2018/8/23/17770046/you-and-sundry-queer-hair-salon-gender.

Beauty CE. "How Your Salon Can Leverage Technology for Success." Beauty Academy, June 28, 2018. https://beautyce.com/how-your-salon-can-leverage-technology-for-success.

Beauty Schools Directory. "Cosmetologist." Retrieved October 1, 2018. https://www.beautyschoolsdirectory.com/faq/cosmetologist.php.

Brown, Rachel. "Skincare Brand Jordan Samuel Is Riding a Direct-to-Consumer Model to $1M in Sales This Year." August 27, 2018. https://www.beautyindependent.com/skincare-brand-jordan-samuel-direct-to-consumer-model.

Bureau of Labor Statistics. "Barbers, Hairstylists, and Cosmetologists." April 13, 2018. https://stats.bls.gov/ooh/personal-care-and-service/barbers-hairstylists-and-cosmetologists.htm.

Evergreen Beauty College. "Top 6 Careers in Cosmetology." Retrieved October 1, 2018. https://www.evergreenbeauty.edu/blog/Top-10-Careers-In-Cosmetology.

Fernbach, Marisa. "Cosmetology: A Beautiful Career." ESSAI, Volume 14, Article 18, Spring 2016. https://dc.cod.edu/cgi/viewcontent.cgi?article=1574&context=essai.

Gilliland, Nikki. "How Beauty Brands Have Evolved Their Influencer Marketing." Econsultancy, June 6, 2018. https://econsultancy.com/how-beauty-brands-have-evolved-their-influencer-marketing.

Hopwood, Claire. "How YouTube Celebrities Are Transforming the Beauty Industry, and What Companies Can Learn from It." Retrieved October 1, 2018. https://www.visioncritical.com/beauty-influencers.

Kestenbaum, Richard. "How the Beauty Industry Is Adapting to Change." *Forbes*, June 19, 2017. https://www.forbes.com/sites/richardkestenbaum

/2017/06/19/how-the-beauty-industry-is-adapting-to-change/#56f5b4953681.

Leisure Jobs. "The Definitive Guide: How to Become a Hairdresser." July 21, 2017. https://www.leisurejobs.com/article/the-definitive-guide-how-to-become-a-hairdresser.

Marshall, Brian. "How Hair Coloring Works." HowStuffWorks. Retrieved November 12, 2018. https://science.howstuffworks.com/innovation/everyday-innovations/hair-coloring.htm.

McKay, Dawn Rosenberg. "Cosmetology Careers: Hair Stylist, Barber, Makeup Artist, Esthetician, and Manicurist." The Balance Careers, December 13, 2017. https://www.thebalancecareers.com/cosmetology-careers-524866.

National-Interstate Council of State Boards of Cosmetology. "About Us." Retrieved November 12, 2018. https://nictesting.org/about-us.

Natural Healers. "5 Job Tips from a Professional Esthetician." Retrieved October 1, 2018. https://www.naturalhealers.com/five-tips-esthetician-interview.

Natural Healers. "Cosmetology." Retrieved November 12, 2018. https://www.naturalhealers.com/cosmetology.

Princeton Review. "A Day in the Life of a Cosmetologist." Retrieved October 1, 2018. https://www.princetonreview.com/careers/45/cosmetologist.

Puff Cuff, The. "Do Cosmetology Schools Teach Curly Hair Care?" April 2018. https://thepuffcuff.com/blogs/news/do-cosmetology-schools-teach-curly-hair-care.

Robinson, Tyra. "What Cosmetology School Did Not Teach Me About My Black Hair." April 4, 2014. https://bglh-marketplace.com/2014/04/what-cosmetology-did-not-teach-me-about-my-black-hair.

Soble, Stacey. "Why Cosmetology Is a Secure Job Choice." Modern Salon, July 6, 2012. https://www.modernsalon.com/article/21233/why-cosmetology-is-a-secure-job-choice.

Trade School Advisor. "Cosmetology and Beauty School." Retrieved November 12, 2018. http://www.tradeschooladvisor.com/cosmetology-school.php.

Index

ABOUT THE AUTHORS

Rachel Given-Wilson has written and edited a number of nonfiction books for teenagers, including the Tech Girls series of books about careers for girls in STEM industries. She lives in Brooklyn, New York, with her family.

Sally Ganchy is an educator and author living in Brooklyn, New York. She has worked with at-risk youth on study skills and career counseling. She has also written books for Rosen about how to use your interests, hobbies, and skills to build a career.

PHOTO CREDITS

Cover Olena Yakobchuk/Shutterstock.com; back cover, pp. 6–7, interior pages (background) Juta/Shutterstock.com; p. 7 (inset) UfaBizPhoto/Shutterstock.com; p. 10 Evgenyrychko /Shutterstock.com; p. 12 Bob Chamberlin/Los Angeles Times /Getty Images; p. 17 antoniodiaz/Shutterstock.com; p. 20 Adam J/Shutterstock.com; p. 23 sirtravelalot/Shutterstock .com; p. 26 Africa Studio/Shutterstock.com; p. 30 Dmytro Zinkevych/Shutterstock.com; p. 31 Lestertair/Shutterstock .com; p. 37 Fashionstock.com/Shutterstock.com; p. 42 Sergei Savinov/Shutterstock.com; p. 44 berezandr/Shutterstock .com; p. 46 Galina Mikhalishina/Shutterstock.com; p. 50 © iStockphoto.com/kali9; p. 51 ND700/Shutterstock.com; p. 55 Nata Sha/Shutterstock.com; p. 58 Monkey Business Images /Shutterstock.com; p. 61 PointImages/Shutterstock.com; p. 64 Astrid Stawiarz/Getty Images.

Design and Layout: Nicole Russo-Duca; Photo Researcher: Nicole DiMella